Junie B., First Grader

Turkeys We Have Loved and Eaten (and Other Thankful Stuff)

Laugh out loud with Junie B. Jones!

Check out Barbara Park's other great books, listed at the end of this book!

BARBARA PARK

Junie B., First Grader®
Turkeys We Have Loved and Eaten (and Other Thankful Stuff)

illustrated by Denise Brunkus

A STEPPING STONE BOOK™

Random House 🏠 New York

For Richard . . .

Text copyright © 2012 by Barbara Park
Jacket art and interior illustrations copyright © 2012 by Denise Brunkus

All rights reserved.
Published in the United States by Random House Children's Books,
a division of Random House, Inc., New York.

Random House and the colophon are registered trademarks and
A Stepping Stone Book and the colophon are trademarks of Random House, Inc.
Junie B., First Grader® stylized design is a registered trademark of Barbara Park,
used under license.

Visit us on the Web!
randomhouse.com/junieb

Educators and librarians, for a variety of teaching tools, visit us at
randomhouse.com/teachers

Library of Congress Cataloging-in-Publication Data
Park, Barbara.
Junie B., first grader : Turkeys we have loved and eaten (and other thankful stuff) /
Barbara Park ; illustrated by Denise Brunkus. — 1st ed.
   p. cm. — (Junie B. Jones ; #28)
"A Stepping Stone book."
Summary: To celebrate the Thanksgiving holiday, Mr. Scary's first grade class prepares
a Thankful List for the school contest, but Junie B. Jones finds it hard to be grateful for
squash or Tattletale May.
ISBN 978-0-375-87063-7 (trade) — ISBN 978-0-375-97063-4 (lib. bdg.) —
ISBN 978-0-307-97435-8 (ebook)
[1. Thanksgiving Day—Fiction. 2. Gratitude—Fiction. 3. Schools—Fiction.
4. Humorous stories.] I. Brunkus, Denise, ill. II. Title.
III. Title: Turkeys we have loved and eaten (and other thankful stuff).
PZ7.P2197Jtv 2012 [Fic]—dc23 2011041350

Printed in the United States of America   10 9 8 7 6 5 4 3 2 1   First Edition

Contents

1

The Contest

Monday

Dear first-grade journal,
   Today is the ~~munth~~ month of
Thanksgiving.
   At Thanksgiving we draw a
lot of turkeys.
   Also, we draw ~~pilgrims~~ Pilgrims and
~~nativ americans~~ Native Americans.
   They are eating at a table
usually.

Both of them seem to enjoy squash.

I do not actually understand Pilgrims ~~pilgrims~~. Their costumes look hottish and sweatish.

This week Room One is making a list of the stuff we are thankful for.

After we get done, we will put our list in a school contest. And the room with the bestest thankful list will win.

Also we are having a Thanksgiving feast on Wednesday. Our families get to come to school.

> Thanksgiving is a lot of
work.
>   Your friend,
>   Junie B., First Grader

I closed my journal and thought about squash.

"Bluck," I said out loud. "I hate squash."

May did a frown.

"Shush, Junie Jones! Can't you see that I am still writing?" she said.

May is the girl who sits next to me.

I am not thankful for her.

Just then, my teacher Mr. Scary stood up at his desk.

"Boys and girls, it's time to get started on our Thankful List for the school contest," he said. "Can everyone please put your journals away?"

"YES!" we shouted back. "YES! YES! YES!"

Then all the children slammed our journals shut very happy.

SLAM! SLAM! BAM! SLAM! BAM! SLAM! SLAM! BAM!

Mr. Scary sucked in his cheeks at us.

He made us open our journals again. And we had to shut them quietly.

It was some sort of slamming lesson, I believe.

Finally, he moved on.

"Okay. Last night's homework was to write down some of the things that you are thankful for," he said.

He picked up a piece of chalk. "Today I

will start printing our Thankful List on the board," he said. "We will work on the list today and tomorrow. And then we will enter it in the school Thankful Contest."

A boy named Roger raised his hand.

"Do we get a prize if we win?" he asked. "I always try harder if there's a prize involved."

Mr. Scary did a frown at him.

"We're not doing this for a *prize*, Roger," he said. "We're doing this to celebrate the things we are thankful for."

Roger tapped his fingers on his desk.

"So is that a yes or a no on the prize?" he asked.

Mr. Scary stood there a minute. Then, all of a sudden, a smile came on his face.

We did not expect that.

"Okay. Fine, Roger," he said. "I was going to let this be a surprise if we won. But yes. There *is* a prize for winning the contest."

All of Room One perked up our ears.

'Cause who doesn't love prizes, of course!

"What is it? What is it?" we called out. "What is the prize? Tell us! Tell us! Tell us!"

Mr. Scary walked back and forth very thinking. He said he was really not supposed to tell us the surprise.

But then ha!

He did a wink!

And he told us anyway!

"The winning class is going to get a *homemade pumpkin pie,*" he said.

He smiled real big.

"And here is the *best* part. The pie will

be made by our very own lunch lady, Mrs. Gladys Gutzman!"

After that, all of the children just sat there. And we didn't say any words.

Instead, our faces turned kind of sickish. And we slumped way down in our chairs.

Finally, I raised my hand.

"Pumpkin pie makes me vomit," I said.

My friend Herbert nodded.

"Me too," he said. "Pumpkin pie makes me vomit, too."

"Me three," said my other friend named Shirley.

"Me four," said a boy named Lennie. "My grandmother's pumpkin pie sits in my mouth like a big wad of goop glop."

Roger looked at Mr. Scary.

"A prize that makes us vomit doesn't seem like much to shoot for," he said.

Mr. Scary sat down at his desk. And rubbed his head.

"Okay. Let's just forget about the pie," he said. "*Really*. This contest is not about winning a pie. This contest is about appreciating all the wonderful things in the world that we are thankful for."

He looked around the room.

"If we're lucky enough to win, the real prize will be how proud we'll feel about doing our best," he said. "A first-grade class has never won this contest before. But I think this class has a great chance. You are definitely the most creative first graders I've ever had."

Roger stood up.

"Now *that* I believe," he said. "My brother Rodney was in your class last year. And Rodney is a dolt."

Mr. Scary closed his eyes. Then he rubbed his head more.

This was not going to be a good morning, probably.

2

Some Thankfuls

Mr. Scary moved on again.

"Okay, boys and girls. Let's really get started now. If you'll please take out your homework papers, we'll begin sharing our ideas. Who would like to go first?"

I quick pulled out my homework.

"ME! ME! ME!" I shouted. "'Cause I have four excellent thankfuls! And I am not even kidding!"

Then I sprang up like a spring. And I started to read my Thankful List.

"First, I am thankful for the turkey I

love at Thanksgiving. Second, I enjoy the gravy. Plus, number three, I am thankful for the kind of cranberry jelly that comes in a can . . . only even when you take it out of the can, it still keeps looking exactly like the can!"

I looked at my teacher. "That stuff is like magic," I said. "I do not know how farmers grow it in that shape."

Mr. Scary stared at me a real long time.

I looked back at my list.

"Oh! And here is my favorite one of all!" I said. "I am thankful for the kind of biscuits that come in a tube. And then you BASH them on the counter! And they come exploding out! And everyone jumps! Plus also, my brother Ollie starts to cry."

I grinned real big. "That is just a fun bunch of biscuits."

My friend Herbert jumped out of his seat.

"I can't believe it, Junie B.! I am thankful for those biscuits, too!" he said.

He quick grabbed his homework page and held it up.

"Look! See? It's right here on my paper! Exploding biscuits!"

After that, me and Herb did a high five. And a low five. And a medium five.

Also, we did a fist bump.

A fist bump is when you knock your knuckles together.

Sometimes it can be painful.

May threw back her head at us.

"Oh no, no, no!" she said. "That can*not* be true. Both of you did *not* write that by yourselves. You copied each other! I know you did! Who in the world is

thankful for exploding biscuits?"

All of the children thought for a second.

Then, one by one, they all started to shout.

"I am!"

"I am!"

"I am, too!" they shouted.

My friend named Sheldon Potts sprang up from his chair.

"Me too!" he called. "One time, I ate SIX exploding biscuits right out of the tube! And they weren't even *cooked* yet!"

All of our eyes popped out of our heads.

'Cause that was the greatest exploding-biscuits story we ever heard.

We looked back at Mr. Scary. His eyes were stuck on Sheldon.

"You're a fascinating little boy, Sheldon Potts," he said.

"Yes, I know. You keep telling me that," said Sheldon.

Mr. Scary smiled. Then he turned to the

board. And he wrote the words THANKFUL LIST.

"Okay, Junie B. How about if you pick out your top two favorites. And we'll start the list off with them."

I stared at my paper very thinking. Then I told him my two favorites. And Mr. Scary printed them on the board:

1. CRANBERRY JELLY IN A CAN
2. EXPLODING BISCUITS

He took a step back.

"Well, just as I thought. We're off to an interesting start," he said.

He turned back to Room One.

"As we continue—if you've brought a long list—please just pick the two things that you are the *most* thankful for. Okay?"

"Okay!" we shouted back.

My friend named Lennie waved his hand to go next.

"All right, Lennie. Your turn. Tell us the *number one* thing in your life that you are the most thankful for."

Lennie yelled it out.

"NIPSY DOODLES!" he said real loud. "I *LOVE* NIPSY DOODLES!"

Mr. Scary's face went funny.

He did not move for a minute.

Then, finally, his eyebrows raised to the top of his head.

"*Nipsy Doodles,* Len?" he repeated kind of quiet. "Really? That's the *number one* thing in your life that you're thankful for? *Nipsy Doodles?*"

Lennie nodded.

Then he checked his homework just to be sure.

"Yes," he said. "Nipsy Doodles is number one."

He smiled. "They are a tasty little cheese snack *unlike any other.*"

Mr. Scary nodded very slow. "Yes. I know, Lennie. I've heard the commercial. And I'm sure they're very tasty. But—just out of curiosity—what is number two on your list?"

Lennie's face started to beam.

"Number two! Rainbow sprinkles!" he yelled.

All of Room One started to clap.

Because the whole world loves rainbow sprinkles, of course!

Mr. Scary didn't move again.

Then finally, he picked up the chalk. And he added Lennie's two thankfuls to the list.

3. NIPSY DOODLES
4. RAINBOW SPRINKLES

He stepped back and took a big breath.

"All rightie. Let's take another look at what we have here so far," he said. "We have four delicious food items, don't we? But just remember . . . there are *other* things to be thankful for, too. Right, boys and girls?"

"Right!" we said.

We thought and thought.

"Like what?" we said.

Mr. Scary chuckled.

"Well, for one thing, in our country we're lucky to have *freedom*," he said.

"Freedom is one reason the Pilgrims came to America."

He looked around the room.

"Did anyone put *freedom* on your Thankful List?"

All of the children looked at their lists.

Then everyone shook their heads no.

Roger stood up again.

"We're only six," he said. "We don't really have any freedom."

He thought for a second. "I'm not even allowed to cross the street by myself."

"Me neither," said Shirley. "I have to stay in my own front yard."

José raised his hand. "I have to go to bed at seven-thirty. And half the time it's still light outside," he said.

Herbert stood up, too. "Well, wait till you hear *this* one! I have to eat cooked carrots or I don't get a cookie after dinner," he said.

Just then, Sheldon slapped his hand on his desk. And he shouted real loud.

"AND I AM FORCED TO TAKE A MULTI-VITAMIN!" he hollered. "Does *THAT* sound like freedom?"

Mr. Scary quick held up his hand.

"Okay, okay. Calm down, everyone! I get it! I get it!" he said.

He looked back at our Thankful List. Then he nodded at us very thoughtful.

"Boys and girls, you are absolutely right. You *are* first graders. And you can be thankful for whatever you want," he said. "This list should be exactly what *you* want it to be. Not me . . . not the contest judges. Not anyone else but *you*."

He smiled.

"Thanks for showing me that," he said.

"You're welcome," we said back.

We are a polite group.

Mr. Scary looked happy again. "All right. Who would like to go next?" he said. "And remember. Whatever you say will be *perfectly fine* with me."

Sheldon jumped up.

"TOILET PAPER! I AM THANKFUL FOR TOILET PAPER!" he shouted.

Mr. Scary's eyes got big and wide.

But he quick snapped out of it. And he printed the words on the board.

"Number five . . . toilet paper," he said.

Sheldon grinned real excited. "We're going to win this contest for sure!" he said.

He did a thumbs-up at Room One.

Then all of us did a thumbs-up back.

Except not actually Mr. Scary.

3

Thankful Bags

Tuesday

Dear first-grade journal,

Today is still the month of Thanksgiving.

But hurray! Hurray!

We are going to have Show and Tell for the whole entire day today!

That is because yesterday, Mr. Scary gave us Thankful

Bags to take home with us. And today we had to bring them back with something we are thankful for.

We are keeping them a secret till Show and Tell.

I brought something that I love very much.

Here is a helpful hint.

It is not my brother Ollie.

Your friend,

Junie B., First Grader

I put down my pencil. And I looked around the room.

All of the children had their Thankful

Bags next to their chairs. Some of the bags looked emptyish. And some of them looked fullish.

My Thankful Bag looked middle-ish.

I picked it up and put it on my desk.

Then I leaned over. And I tapped on May's arm.

"My Thankful Bag is middle-ish," I said real pleasant.

May did not pay attention to me.

I tapped on her arm again.

"You are probably wondering what is in my bag. But I cannot tell you. On account of it has to stay a surprise until Show-and-Tell," I said.

May turned her back on me.

This time, I tapped on her head.

"Helpful hint: It is not my brother Ollie," I said.

Just then, May exploded out of her seat!
And she tattletaled real loud!

"MR. SCARY! MR. SCARY! JUNIE
JONES WILL NOT STOP BOTHERING
ME!" she hollered.

Mr. Scary frowned his eyebrows at me.

I waved my fingers very friendly.

"Hello. How are you today? I am fine," I said. "I was just showing May my Thankful Bag."

I held it up in the air.

"It is middle-ish," I said.

Mr. Scary kept on frowning.

I put my bag on my desk. And I folded my hands very polite.

"Okay. I guess that about wraps it up," I said.

Mr. Scary got a teensy smile on his face.

Sometimes he enjoys me, I believe.

Pretty soon, he stood up at his desk. And he clapped his loud hands together.

"Okay, boys and girls. It's time to get started with our very special day of Show-and-Tell!" he said. "Please put your journals away and arrange your chairs in a circle."

We slammed our journals shut.

SLAM! SLAM! BAM! SLAM! BAM! SLAM! SLAM! BAM!

Mr. Scary sucked in his cheeks at us.

We quick opened our journals again. And we shut them very quiet.

After that, we put our chairs in a circle. And we got ready for a *whole entire day* of Show-and-Tell.

"Woo-hoo!" I said to Herbert. "This is a dream come true! A whole entire day with no learning!"

Herb laughed and clapped. "I wish every day had no learning," he said.

"Me too!" I said. "If every day had no learning, school would be a lot more popular."

May butted in to our conversation.

"Well, I am *thankful* for learning," she said. "There is nothing I like better than learning . . . learning . . . learning."

After that, she started skipping around her chair.

I did a glare at her.

"Here is a suggestion," I said. "Why don't you skip on home?"

May stuck out her tongue at me.

There was no need for that, I believe.

Just then, Mr. Scary clapped his hands again. "Okay, everyone. Make sure you have your Thankful Bags at your chairs . . . and please take a seat."

All of us got our bags and sat down.

"Good job," he said. "It looks like we're ready to begin. I can't wait to see what kind of wonderful things you're thankful for."

He pointed to Roger.

"Roger, would you like to start us off?" he said.

Roger's face looked sickish. "Why?" he said. "Why me? I didn't even raise my hand."

Mr. Scary smiled. "I know you didn't, Roger," he said. "I just thought you might like to start us off, that's all."

Roger did a gulp. "Oh," he said. "Well . . . um . . . I wouldn't."

Mr. Scary stopped smiling.

"Okay. It wasn't really a *question*, Roger," he explained. "I would like you to go first."

Roger's face got sweaty on it.

He just kept sitting there.

Mr. Scary crossed his arms at him. "Roger?" he said. "We're waiting."

Finally, Roger did a big deep breath.

Then he stood up real slow. And he picked up his Thankful Bag.

It looked emptyish.

"Um . . . well, uh . . . mostly, I'm just thankful for this Thankful Bag," he said.

He held it out in front of him. And he gave it a little shake.

"I don't know why I like this bag so much. But I'm just really, really thankful for it," he said.

He did a pause.

"The end," he said.

Then he quick sat back down.

Mr. Scary frowned. "Really, Roger? Seriously?" he said. "In your whole life, you're only thankful for the plastic bag I gave you yesterday? That's *it*?"

Roger stood up again.

"Uh, well, no. I mean, I'm thankful for other stuff, too," he said.

Mr. Scary raised his eyebrows. "Like?"

Roger's face got stress in it. "Like . . . like . . ."

He quick looked all around himself. Then all of a sudden, he stretched out the bottom of his T-shirt.

"Like this T-shirt I am wearing," he said. "I am very, very thankful for this T-shirt."

Roger's face got sweatier.

"This T-shirt is . . . um . . ."

He looked at it harder.

". . . white," he said finally.

Mr. Scary nodded real slow. "Yes," he said. "We can see that, Roger."

Roger kept stretching his shirt.

Then he turned up the bottom. And he read us the tag.

"*Machine-wash, warm. Lay flat to dry,*" he read.

After that, he stretched out the back of the neck. And he read us *that* tag, too.

"*Boys' size six to eight,*" he read.

"*Made . . . in . . .*"

Mr. Scary quick held up his hand.

"That's *enough*, Roger," he said very sternish.

Roger kept on standing there.

". . . *Honduras,*" he said.

Mr. Scary snapped his loud fingers.

Roger sat down.

Show-and-Tell was not off to a good start.

4

Diving

Mr. Scary stared at Roger a real long time.

He said they would *talk about this later.*

Talk about this later is the school word for getting yelled at when there's more time.

Roger slumped way down in his seat.

After that, Mr. Scary looked back at the class.

"Okay, everyone. We're going to continue now," he said. "But this time, please raise your hand if you actually brought something to show."

Lucille sprang out of her chair.

"I DID! I DID!" she hollered. "I BROUGHT THE BEST THING YOU EVER SAW!"

Then she reached down. And she pulled a big, giant purse out of her Thankful Bag.

"Wait till you see *this*, children!" she said. "I brought something that everyone in the *whole world* is thankful for! And I have LOTS and LOTS of it!"

After that, she turned the big, giant purse upside down.

And wowie wow wow!

Out came . . .

"MONEY!" shouted Lucille. "MONEY! MONEY! MONEY! I AM THANKFUL FOR MONEY!"

Room One did a gasp at that sight.

Then all of our mouths fell open at once.

And our eyes got bigger and bigger.

And then . . . *BAM!*
WE DIVED FOR IT!

"MONEY!" we hollered. "MONEY! MONEY! MONEY!"

I started to grab.

"AND IT'S THE *PAPER KIND*!" I yelled.

Lucille laughed real happy.

Then she turned her Thankful Bag inside out. And more money fell out on top of us!

"WHEE! WOOO-HOOO! YIPPEE!" we hollered.

Mr. Scary was hollering, too, I think. But it is hard to hear your teacher when you are money-diving.

Finally, he raised his voice to a louder level.

It was the level that means business.

"GO BACK TO YOUR SEATS!" he hollered. *"NOW!"*

Everyone stopped grabbing. And they

hurried back to their seats speedy fast.

Except for not actually me.

Instead, I kept on sitting on the floor. 'Cause I had a teensy problem.

Mr. Scary glared his eyes at me.

"Junie B. Jones? Did you *hear* me? I said, go back to your seat."

I nodded real nervous.

"Yes," I said. "Only I have a teensy problem."

I pointed at his shoe. "You're actually standing on a fiver. And so if you could just lift up this one shoe right here, I can get my money and be on my way."

I tapped on the foot he should lift.

Then I waited and waited for it to move. But it did not actually budge.

Instead . . . YIKES!

I felt *myself* getting lifted off the floor!

And I got carried right back to my seat!

Mr. Scary sat me in my chair.

I smiled real twitchy. And I smoothed my skirt.

"Okey-doke," I said. "I believe I will just sit here now and behave myself."

Mr. Scary kept on standing there.

I waved my fingers at him.

"All rightie, then. Have a good day," I said.

He took some deep breaths.

Deep breaths are what teachers do to keep from screaming.

Room One stayed quiet as a mouse.

I could hear Mr. Scary's nose whistle. But now was not the time to tell him he needed a tissue, probably.

Finally, he finished breathing.

Then he picked up Lucille's big, giant

purse. And he went around the circle. And he made all of us put her money back.

Sheldon hung his head.

"I'm sorry," he said. "Free money makes me cuckoo."

Herb nodded. "Me too," he said. "Especially the *paper* kind. At my house, I don't even get an allowance."

"Me neither," said Roger. "My parents expect me to live at home for *free*."

Lennie rolled his eyes. "Oh. Well, I get a whopping quarter for taking out the trash. Seriously. That's *it*. One quarter."

He threw his hands in the air. "I mean, why even *bother*?"

Mr. Scary snapped his fingers.

That means *knock it off*.

After that, all of us stayed quiet while Mr. Scary went to the board.

He stood there very thinking.

Then finally, he picked up the chalk. And he added MONEY to our Thankful List.

After he finished, he took Lucille by the hand. And he walked her to the door.

"Boys and girls, Lucille and I are going to take her money to the office for safekeeping," he said. "But while we are gone, I want you all to stay in your seats. And I want you to think *very, very hard* about what just happened here."

He narrowed his eyes at us.

"I think we all know that Lucille's family is wealthy. And we are all very happy for her. But there are lots of other things to be thankful for besides money. Right, Lucille?" he said.

"Right," she said back.

She shook her head around in the air. "I

am also thankful for my shiny, gleaming hair."

Then she kept on shaking it and shaking it until Mr. Scary said, "Please stop."

He looked at her. "Believe it or not, Lucille, there are plenty of people who don't have money *or* shiny hair. But they are still very happy."

Lucille fluffed herself.

"That's just nuts," she said.

Mr. Scary pulled her out the door.

5

Talking It Over

I did what Mr. Scary said.

I stayed in my seat.

And I thought very hard about *what just happened here*.

First, I tapped on my chin.

Then I scratched my head. And I strained and strained my brain.

But nothing actually came to me.

Finally, I tapped on Herbert.

"Okay. I give up. What just happened here?" I asked. "Why is Mr. Scary so mad at us?"

Herb did a shrug.

"I'm not really sure," he said. "We dived in a pile of money. Who wouldn't do that?"

May jumped up and pointed to herself.

"*I* wouldn't, *that's* who!" she said. "I did *not* dive in the money pile. Instead, I walked around the edges with dignity. And I picked up whatever money squeezed out."

Herb looked curious at her.

"How much money squeezed out?"

May stood there a minute.

"None," she said.

"Exactly," said Herb.

May sat back down.

Herb looked at the board and sighed.

"I have a feeling that Mr. Scary really hates our Thankful List."

May threw her head back.

"Of *course* he hates our Thankful List!"

she said. "Just look how stupid it is!"

She hurried to the board.

And she read each item out loud.

1. CRANBERRY JELLY IN A CAN
2. EXPLODING BISCUITS
3. NIPSY DOODLES
4. RAINBOW SPRINKLES
5. TOILET PAPER
6. MONEY

I scratched my head again.

"I don't see the problem," I said. "I think we have a nice little assortment there."

May stamped her foot.

"It's stupid, Junie Jones! Stupid, stupid, stupid!" she said. "Who in the world is thankful for toilet paper?"

Sheldon raised his hand.

"I am!" he said. "My grampa Ned Potts says that toilet paper was one of the greatest inventions in history. Especially after they put that little cardboard rollie thing inside."

I nodded. "Yes," I said. "That cardboard rollie thing is a genius. If you put some string through it, it makes a lovely necklace for Mother's Day."

José jumped up. "PLUS, if you have two of them, you can make binoculars!" he said. "I make binoculars and spy on my sister. And they really, *really* work!"

May did a huffy breath at us.

"Well, I don't care *what* you guys say. My mother, Mrs. Mary Murkee, says our list from yesterday is ridiculous. She says children are *never* thankful for the right stuff. And so that's how come she started a brand-new Thankful List for us."

She reached in her pocket and pulled out the list. "My mother says if we use *this* list, we will win the contest for sure."

She unfolded it. "Who wants to hear it? Who wants to hear the brand-new list my mother started?"

No one raised their hand.

May read it anyway.

OUR THANKFUL LIST
BY ROOM ONE
NUMBER 1:

Room One is thankful for our mothers, who cover us in blankets of warm, fuzzy love and make our hearts overflow with joy bubbles.

NUMBER 2:

Room One is thankful for the happy sound of our mothers' laughter as it tinkles through the air and melts like musical snow crystals in our ears.

NUMBER 3:

Room One is thankful for May.

The End.

May looked up and grinned.

"I added that last one myself. But I think it fits right in," she said.

She folded her list up again. And she skipped back to her seat.

At first, Room One did not say any words. We just stared at each other with curious eyes.

Then finally, Lennie spoke up.

"I think we should stick with the Nipsy Doodles," he said.

All of the children got relief in our faces.

"Yes, yes! Me too! Me too!" we said.

May's face looked angry at us.

She stomped her foot again.

"I *knew* this would happen! I told Mother you people wouldn't listen!"

She covered her head with her sweater.

All of us ignored her.

We looked at the board some more.

Then, all of a sudden, Shirley clapped her hands together.

"Hey! Wait! I've got an idea! Let's put something on the list that *every* grown-up likes! That way Mr. Scary will be happier with us. And maybe we'll get more votes from the grown-up judges!"

I thought for a second.

"Yeah, but what does *every* grown-up like, Shirley?" I asked. "I don't even have a clue."

Shirley thought for a second, too. Then she sprang right up.

"I got it! It just came to me! NATURE!" she said. "Every grown-up loves nature! They love flowers and trees and mountains and oceans and other junk like that."

She clapped her hands. "Plus every grown-up I know loves cute little forest animals," she said. "Let's put *that* one on the board! Let's put cute little forest animals!"

She ran to get the chalk.

Sheldon quick stood up.

"No, Shirley. Wait!" he called. "My aunt Bunny is a grown-up. But *she* doesn't love forest animals. Last summer, she had a run-in with a raccoon. It jumped on her head. And then it just sat there like a hat."

He did a shiver. "For a very long time, I mean," he said.

Herb nodded. "My mother doesn't like forest animals, either," he said. "Last year, we went to the state park. And a squirrel spit on her when she handed him a Frito," he said.

He looked disturbed. "She said a bad word. We have it on video."

Lennie raised his hand. "My grandmother doesn't even like the *forest*," he said. "Last year, we took her camping, and she got her foot stuck in a pork-and-beans can."

He covered his face very embarrassed. "She said she was trying to make *camp slippers*."

After that, all the other children started telling terrible nature stories, too.

Shirley hung down her head and went back to her seat.

I leaned over and patted her.

"Don't feel bad, Shirley," I said. "Being thankful is just harder than we thought."

"Sí," said José.

He held up his Thankful Bag. "I brought

in our TV remote. But now that seems estúpido," he said.

He looked over at Roger. "I wish I had forgotten mine, like you did, Rog," he said.

Roger squirmed in his chair. "Well, um . . . I didn't really *forget* mine, José," he said. "I brought in a can of whipped cream. But I squirted it in my mouth before school started."

José smiled. "Who wouldn't?" he said.

Just then, we heard feet in the hall.

"Shh! Shh! Mr. Scary is coming! Mr. Scary is coming!" we whispered to each other.

Then Room One got speedy quiet.

And Mr. Scary and Lucille walked right in the door.

And ha! We did not get caught talking!

Mr. Scary took Lucille back to her chair.

She fluffed her shiny hair. And she did a spin.

"I didn't even get in trouble," she said. "All I had to do was put my money in the safe. And I had to promise not to throw dollars at poor people."

Mr. Scary frowned his eyebrows.

"I don't really think that was our message, Lucille," he said. "We talked about not bragging. And we said that having money doesn't make you *better* than anyone else. Remember that?"

Lucille fluffed some more.

"Nope," she said.

Then she skipped in a circle. And she twirled herself into her chair.

Mr. Scary looked at the rest of us. "Boys

and girls, I'm sure you all know that diving for money was not a good decision. Correct?" he said.

"Correct!" we shouted.

We did not really believe that. But sometimes it is just better to shout *correct*.

"Okay, good," he said. "Then, if all of you promise to behave like ladies and gentlemen, we'll get on with Show-and-Tell."

"We promise! We promise!" we shouted.

Mr. Scary smiled.

We relaxed our shoulders.

When a teacher smiles, everything feels better.

6

Something in Common

Mr. Scary roamed his eyes around the circle.

"Okay, let's get started again. Who has brought something so, so special that you can't wait *one more second* to show us?"

"ME!" I shouted. "ME, ME, ME!"

"NO, ME! ME! ME!" shouted May, even louder.

Then she quick jumped up. And she reached into her Thankful Bag.

And so I quick jumped up. And I reached into *my* Thankful Bag, too!

And then *BOOM!*

Both of us pulled out our thankful items at the *very same time*!

And I could not believe my eyeballs, I tell you!

On account of me and May brought the *same* thankful item from home!

And here is the shockingest part of all.

They were the *exact same stuffed elephants*!

It still takes my breathing away to think about that.

'Cause me and May are *nothing* alike. And so how can we be thankful for the same elephants?

Both of us kept staring at this terrible situation. We could not even say any words.

Mr. Scary leaned back in his chair and smiled. "Well, this is very interesting, isn't it?" he said.

His smile got bigger.

"I actually *love* this, girls," he said. "It just shows us that even when people are quite different from each other, they can still have things in common."

He stood up.

"That's what happened with the Native Americans and the Pilgrims, remember?" he asked. "Even though they were different from each other, they were thankful for many of the same things. And that allowed them to become friends."

I quick raised my hand.

"Yeah, only May and I are *not* friends, Mr. Scary. Plus I don't even *get* Pilgrims," I said. "Their costumes look hottish and sweatish."

May stepped in front of me.

"Well, I *love* Pilgrims!" she said. "I wish

I was wearing hot, sweaty Pilgrim clothes right now."

I did a huff at her.

"If I was an Indian, I would not eat squash with you," I said.

Mr. Scary laughed.

"See, girls? See how different you are?" he said. "But look! You're both thankful for the same little toy."

I frowned my eyes at that comment.

"Philip Johnny Bob is not a *little toy,* Mr. Scary," I said, real annoyed. "Philip Johnny Bob is the *bestest stuffed-animal friend* I've ever had."

May nodded. "And *my* elephant is my best stuffed-animal friend, too," she said. "His name is Police Sergeant Chuck. And I have known him since my mother brought him home from the store."

She held him up for everyone to see.

"My mother made this little police uniform for him. See it, everyone?" she said. "He has a little police jacket. And a little police hat. And a shiny little police badge."

She looked at Philip Johnny Bob and made a face.

"Police Sergeant Chuck does not have *patches* sewed on him like Junie Jones's old elephant," she said. "Junie Jones's old elephant has been all torn and ripped."

I made squinty eyes at her.

"Yeah, only here is a news flash, madam," I said. "In Mother Nature, elephants do *not* wear police uniforms. In Mother Nature, Police Sergeant Chuck would look like a nitwit."

Philip Johnny Bob laughed out loud.

Ha! Good one, Junie B.! he said. *Plus I LOVE my patches.*

Me and Philip have the same actual talking voice.

I hugged him real tight. "Yes, I know you do, Phil," I said. "Plus the only reason you have patches is because sometimes—when you and I wrestle—I accidentally throw you too high in the air. And then you land on the ceiling fan. And I have to turn up the fan speed to get you off. And then you fly across the room. And you land on the pointy living room lamp."

Philip hugged me back.

But I love riding on the ceiling fan, he said. *It's fun.*

I smoothed his softy ears.

"I know it is, Phil. That's how come I

throw you up there whenever Mother is out of the room," I said.

May did a gasp.

"Friends do *not* throw friends on ceiling fans!" she said. "Riding on a ceiling fan is even against the law, I bet!"

Police Sergeant Chuck nodded real fast. *Yes! Yes! I bet I could arrest him for that!* he said.

Chuck and May have the same voice, too.

May smiled. "Yes! I bet you could, too!" she said.

And so Police Sergeant Chuck got right in Phil's face. And he said, *I'm taking you to jail, Peanut Butter and Johnny!*

Then he bopped Phil in the head with his trunk.

And so Philip bopped him back.

And then *BAM!*

They wrestled all around in the air!

And they bopped and flopped and socked and thunked.

Plus also, they chased each other around the Show-and-Tell circle.

All of Room One laughed and clapped.

It was very joyful.

Then—"WHOA! WHOA! WHOA!"

A loud voice interrupted all the excitement.

"KNOCK IT OFF, YOU TWO!" it said. "RIGHT NOW!"

Everyone looked up.

Mr. Scary's face was reddish and maddish. Also, his hair looked wildish and spriggish.

Me and May stopped running speedy fast.

Phil and Chuck stopped running, too.

Mr. Scary ran his fingers through his wildish hair. "What do you girls think you're doing?" he said.

Me and May looked nervous at each other.

We rocked back and forth on our feet. And we tried to think real fast.

"Um . . . well . . . let's see," I said very shaky. "What do we think we're doing, May?"

May's voice was shaky, too. "Uh . . . hmm, well, right now, we think Police Sergeant Chuck is chasing Peanut Butter and Johnny. Because Peanut Butter and Johnny is running away from him."

She glanced her eyes at me. "Right, Junie Jones?"

I nodded my fastest.

"Yes," I said. "That is because Peanut Butter and Johnny does not want to be arrested by a nitwit elephant in a police suit."

Just then, Police Sergeant Chuck looked shocked at me.

Hey! he shouted. *You can't say that!*

Then he turned around to May.

And he hollered, *Cuff him!*

And before I knew it, May pulled some teensy handcuffs out of Chuck's jacket. And she tried to put them on Philip Johnny Bob.

But ha!

Philip was way too fast for her! And he ducked out of the way.

Then me and Phil started to run again.

Only this time, Mr. Scary stepped in front of us.

And he took Philip right out of my hands!

Plus he took Police Sergeant Chuck out of May's hands, too.

After that, he snapped his loud fingers for us to sit down.

And so both of us sat.

End of joy.

7

Stinky

Mr. Scary put our elephants on his desk.

He did a sigh at May and me.

Then he went to the board. And he thought for a minute.

"Okay, you two. I'm going to put your friends on our Thankful List. But I am *not* happy with the way you behaved just now. And we will definitely talk about this later," he said.

Roger looked over at us. "Welcome to the club," he said.

Mr. Scary frowned at him. Then he added our elephants to the list on the board.

After he finished, he stood back. And he read the list out loud.

1. CRANBERRY JELLY IN A CAN
2. EXPLODING BISCUITS
3. NIPSY DOODLES
4. RAINBOW SPRINKLES
5. TOILET PAPER
6. MONEY
7. PHILIP JOHNNY BOB
8. POLICE SERGEANT CHUCK

"Well," he said. "This list might not win us a pumpkin pie, but it certainly is unusual, isn't it?"

I smiled and nodded. "Yes," I said. "Plus we don't even *care* about the pumpkin pie, remember that? Pumpkin pie makes us vomit."

Mr. Scary looked at me.

"Yes. I do remember that, Junie B. But thank you for mentioning it again," he said.

"Not a problem," I said.

Just then, Lennie waved his hand real urgent.

"Ooooh! Ooooh! Here is a little pumpkin pie trick I learned last Thanksgiving," he said. "I don't actually *swallow* the pie. Instead, I just keep it in my mouth until my grandmother *thinks* I swallowed it. And then I run into the bathroom. And I spit it in the sink."

Mr. Scary closed his eyes. "Good to know, Len," he said.

Lucille jumped up and did a fluff.

"I have a pumpkin pie trick, too," she said. "*First,* I put the pie on my fork. *Then* I plop it in the rich, expensive napkin that is on my lap. And I wad it all up. And then I skip it into the kitchen. And I give it to our rich, expensive chef."

She did a few more fluffs.

"After that, I don't know what happens to it," she said. Then she spun herself back into her chair.

All of Room One thought for a minute. Then other children started calling out pumpkin pie tricks, too. And so Mr. Scary quick held up his hand.

"Stop. Please, boys and girls. I *get* it that you don't like pumpkin pie," he said. "It's just that I don't want anyone to be disappointed if we don't win the contest."

All of us looked around at each other.

Then Herbert raised his hand.

"But see . . . we think that *you're* the one who is disappointed, Mr. Scary," he said. "May said that you hate our Thankful

List because we're not being thankful for the right stuff."

May popped up from her seat.

"I *tried* to get them to change it, Mr. Scary," she said. "My mother, Mrs. Mary Murkee, made us a brand-new Thankful List you would really like. But everyone wanted to stay with Nipsy Doodles and exploding biscuits. So it is *their* fault we won't win that disgusting pie for you!"

I looked at her real angry. "I would like to explode a biscuit on your head right now," I said.

Then everyone laughed.

Except not May. Plus not Mr. Scary.

He did a glare at me.

"Whoops. Sorry," I said. "That was very too harsh."

Mr. Scary turned back to the class.

"Boys and girls, please believe me. I will *not* be disappointed if we don't win the pumpkin pie," he said. "I promise."

He paused for a second.

Then his face got a little smile on it. And he made his voice real secret.

"Shh. Don't tell anyone, okay? But I don't like pumpkin pie, either," he whispered.

Room One got very quiet.

Then HA!

All of us started laughing at once!

'Cause sometimes teachers are just like normal people, almost!

Mr. Scary looked at the clock. "Okay, everyone. I think we have time for two more thankful items before lunch. Who would like to go next?" he said.

Shirley raised her hand.

"I would! I would!" she said. "I have

been waiting to show this all morning!"

Then she quick stood up. And she reached into her Thankful Bag.

And she pulled out a box of—

"SNAUSAGES!" she shouted. "I AM THANKFUL FOR SNAUSAGES!"

Mr. Scary raised his eyebrows. "Snausages, Shirley?" he asked. *"Really?"*

"Yes," said Shirley. "Snausages are little sausage snacks for dogs. And last year—when my dog Stinky got sick—he wouldn't take his pills to get better. So my mother stuck his pills in Snausages. And then Stinky ate them! And he got better! And so Snausages saved Stinky's life!"

"Whoa!" said Herbert.

"Wow!" said Lennie. "That is a power-ful Snausage story, Shirley."

"I know it," she said. "We are trying to

get it made into a major motion picture starring Stinky."

After that, she passed around a Snausage snack. Plus also, she passed around a picture of Stinky.

Mr. Scary went to the board. And he wrote number nine.

9. SNAUSAGES

Then he winked at Shirley. And he added number ten.

10. STINKY

Shirley beamed from ear to ear.
All of Room One beamed, too.
The day was getting happier.

8

Three Squeezes

Mr. Scary checked the clock again.

"Okay. It's time for our last thankful item before lunch," he said. "Shirley's Snausage story was so nice. I'm wondering if anyone else has an animal you're thankful for."

Sheldon's hand shot up like a rocket.

"I do! I do, Mr. Scary! I have *three* animals I am thankful for! And guess what? I got my picture taken with every single one of them!"

He quick leaned down to his Thankful Bag. And he started searching through it.

He stopped to glance up.

"And here's the part that you're *really* going to love," he said. "*All* of the animals are Thanksgiving animals, Mr. Scary! All of them are *turkeys*!"

Mr. Scary looked happy at that news. "Turkeys?" he said. "No kidding, Sheldon? That's great!"

"I know it!" said Sheldon. "My uncle Vern has turkeys at his house. And he took pictures of me with the three that I love the most."

Mr. Scary smiled real big.

"This is *perfect,* Sheldon! I didn't even know that your uncle Vern was a turkey farmer."

Sheldon looked puzzled. "He's not," he said. "Uncle Vern and Aunt Bunny live out in the woods."

He did a pause.

"They moved out there to get away from the law," he said.

Mr. Scary cleared his throat real nervous. "Yes. Well, um . . . that's fine, Sheldon. But that story is really none of our business," he said.

Well, I think it's our business! shouted a loud voice. *I think he should be arrested!*

All of our eyes turned to May.

Her face looked shocked at us.

"Don't look at *me*! I didn't say that! It was *him*!" she said.

Then she quick pointed to Police Sergeant Chuck on Mr. Scary's desk.

Mr. Scary rolled his eyes very annoyed.

He told May to button her lips.

She started to sputter. "But . . . but . . . but . . ."

Mr. Scary snapped his fingers at her. Then he turned back to Sheldon.

"Please forgive that interruption, Sheldon," he said. "I really can't wait to see your turkey pictures! I've seen wild turkeys when I've been hiking. But I've never been close enough to get a picture."

"Really?" said Sheldon. "That's odd. It's easy to get turkey pictures at Uncle Vern's. He brings them right inside his camper."

Mr. Scary's face went funny. But he didn't say any words.

Then, all of a sudden, Sheldon found the pictures he was looking for in his Thankful Bag. And his whole face lighted up.

"I found them! Here they are! Here are

the pictures of me and my three favorite turkeys at Uncle Vern's!" he said.

He took them out and put them in order.

"Number one is Gary Gobbles.

"Number two is Harry Gobbles.

"And number three is Larry Gobbles!"

He smiled real big at that one.

"Larry was from last year," he said. "He is the turkey I loved the most."

He jumped up and held Larry's picture for all of us to see.

"Look, everyone. See him? See Larry?"

We leaned in closer.

Then all of our faces went funny.

Plus Mr. Scary's face went funny again, too.

"Oh, uh, well . . . this isn't what we expected, Sheldon," he said. "This isn't a picture of a *wild* turkey in the woods, is it?"

He did a hard swallow. "This is a picture of a *cooked* turkey . . . on your *plate* . . . and you're *eating* it."

Sheldon nodded real happy.

"Yes," he said. "I know. At Thanksgiving, we take pictures of the delicious turkeys we have loved and eaten. And this is Larry from last year."

He looked curious at our teacher.

"Don't *you* take pictures of *your* Thanksgiving dinners?" he asked.

Mr. Scary thought a minute.

"Well, yes. Now that I think about it, we *do*, Sheldon. We *do* take pictures of our Thanksgiving meals," he said.

Sheldon smiled at Larry again.

"Larry was my favorite," he said. "Look. See? Uncle Vern gave me the drumstick. In our family, it is an *honor* to get a Thanksgiving drumstick."

Sheldon stood up straight and tall. "The drumstick is what a *king* gets," he said real proud.

I thought about that.

"I've *never* gotten a drumstick," I said real disappointed.

"Me neither," said my friend Herbert.

"My mother says if she gives me the drumstick, I'll slop it on the tablecloth."

Sheldon beamed. "My uncle Vern didn't care if I slopped it," he said. "He just told me, 'Enjoy it, Sheldon!'"

Sheldon grinned real big.

"And here is something *else* I love about Thanksgiving at Uncle Vern's," he said. "Before we eat, we all hold hands around the table. And we squeeze each other's hands three times."

He joined his two hands together. And he showed us how to squeeze.

"One squeeze . . . two squeezes . . . three squeezes," he said. "Three squeezes stand for three special words."

He looked around the room. "Can anyone guess what the three special words are?" he asked.

Room One thought and thought. But we could not come up with the three special words.

Finally, Mr. Scary put his hand on Sheldon's shoulder. And he smiled down at him.

"*I love you,*" he said.

Sheldon stood there for a second.

Then he smiled kind of shy.

"Well, uh . . . I love you, too," he said. "But can you guess what words the three squeezes stand for?"

Mr. Scary stood there very frozen.

He did not make any more guesses.

And so, finally, Sheldon blurted it out.

"HAPPY TURKEY DAY!" he said. "The three squeezes stand for HAPPY TURKEY DAY! And so that's how come we always name the turkeys! 'Cause they make our Thanksgiving Day happy and delicious!

And we don't ever want to forget them!"

I thought that over in my head.

Room One thought it over, too.

Then, all at once, we started to clap.

'Cause that is the nicest way to remember a turkey that we ever heard of!

Sheldon looked at his Thanksgiving pictures again. "Good old Larry from last year," he said kind of quiet.

Mr. Scary smiled.

Then he walked to the board.

And he picked up his chalk.

And he wrote it on the board.

11. GOOD OLD LARRY FROM LAST YEAR

Room One clapped some more.

Good old Sheldon Potts.

9

Socks and Other Surprises

Wednesday

Dear first-grade journal,

Today is the day for the Thanksgiving feast in Room One.

All of the children had to dress up like Pilgrims or Native Americans at the first Thanksgiving.

And so that is how come I

told Mother . . . DO NOT MAKE
ME A PILGRIM COSTUME.
AND I MEAN IT!

I could not have been louder,
by the way.

Only what do you know?

Mother said she forgot I told
her that. Plus also, she gave
the costume job to my grandma
Helen Miller.

And so—big surprise—this
morning Helen brought the
costume to my house.

AND OH NO! OH NO!

IT WAS A STUPID PILGRIM
DRESS!

I did a ~~shreek~~ shriek at that thing!
Then I ran down the hall . . .
and out the back door. And I
hid behind the trash can next
to the steps.
But Mother found me speedy
fast. And then me and her had
a little tussle.
And what do you know?
Now I am sitting in my chair
at school.
AND I AM WEARING A
STUPID PILGRIM DRESS!
This is the worstest day of
my entire school career.

Your friend,
Junie B., I DO NOT
WANT TO BE A PILGRIM
AND I MEAN IT!

I slumped in my seat real glum.

Then *BAM!*

The morning got even worse!

On account of May came running into the room. And she was dressed like a Native American Indian girl!

And that is what *I* wanted to be!

I slumped lower in my chair.

May hurried down our row. And she poked me in the arm.

"Hello, Junie Jones. Hello," she said. "Look at the Thanksgiving costume my mother made for me! I am a Native American Indian girl!"

She poked me again. "Look how *great* this costume is! Look at the fringe on the bottom of my dress! Look at the beads around the collar! Look at my cute moccasins! Look at the long braid in my hair!"

I turned my face away from her.

"Look at the back of my head," I said.

May ran around in front of me.

"Guess what my name is, Junie Jones? My name is Chief May—Chief of Everybody. And I will be bossing around the Native Americans at the feast today. Plus I will be bossing around the Pilgrims, too."

After that, she looked me over.

"Hmm, let's see . . . it looks like you are a little Pilgrim girl," she said. "A little

Pilgrim girl is not the chief of anyone, is she? A little Pilgrim girl is just a . . . *girl*."

She did a smirk.

"What is your name, little Pilgrim girl?" she asked. "Do you have a name?"

I made squinty eyes at her.

"My name is Get Out of My Face, Chief Nutball," I said back.

I do not know where I came up with that great name. These things just come to me.

May frowned her eyebrows. "I think your name is Pilgrim Grouchy!" she said.

After that, she swung her long braid in my face. And she sat down in her seat.

Just then, Mr. Scary came hurrying into the room. He had been talking to someone in the hall.

His face beamed at our costumes.

"Boys and girls, you look *so great* in your Thanksgiving outfits!" he said. "We are going to have the best time with our families today."

He held up one finger.

"And don't forget! Today the office is going to announce who won the Thankful Contest."

I did a loud groan.

"Great," I grouched. "I'm already hottish and sweatish. Now all I need to do is win a pie and vomit."

Suddenly, a loud noise interrupted my grouching.

TAP! TAP! TAP!

TAP! TAP! TAP!

It was coming from the hall outside Room One.

All of the children ran to see.

And WHOA!

It was Principal!

And he was hammering a *nail* in our door with his shoe!

All of our mouths came open at that sight.

"I cannot believe my eyeballs," I said real shocked. "If I nailed a hole in our door, I would get sent to Principal's office."

I looked at Mr. Scary. "You know that's true, by the way," I said. "I have been sent for way less than that."

Sheldon raised his hand.

"How come you're doing that, Principal?" he asked. "How come you're nailing a hole in our door with your shoe?"

Just then, his eyes glanced down at Principal's sock foot.

"Whoa! What kind of socks do you have

on there?" he asked real curious.

Sheldon quick got on his hands and knees and looked closer.

He raised his eyebrows. "Are those kneesocks?" he said. "My grandpa Ned Potts wears kneesocks."

I got on my hands and knees, too.

"My grampa Frank Miller wears those kind of socks, too," I said. "We call them *old-man socks.*"

Principal's face looked embarrassed at us.

He said to please get away from his sock foot. Then he quick put his shoe back on.

After that, he did a deep breath to settle down.

Then, surprise! Surprise! He reached into his pocket.

And he pulled out a giant blue ribbon.

And he hung it right on the door nail!

"CONGRATULATIONS TO YOU, ROOM ONE!" he said real happy. "YOU WON FIRST PLACE IN THIS YEAR'S THANKFUL CONTEST!"

All of Room One stood very still for a minute.

That is called *we were in a daze,* I believe.

Then *BOOM!*

We jumped! And clapped! And danced! And yelled!

"WE WON! WE WON! WE WON!" we yelled.

Mr. Scary's face looked thrilled at us.

"I *knew* you could do it!" he said. "I *told* you that you were a special group!"

Me and Herbert linked our arms together. And we skipped in a happy circle.

"WE WON, JUNIE B.!" hollered Herb. "WE WON A GIANT FIRST PLACE BLUE RIBBON! AND A BIG PUMPKIN PIE!"

Then *SCREEEEECH!*

All of our skipping came to a stop.

'Cause we remembered the vomit part, that's why.

Herb and I looked sickish at each other.

Then all of the other children looked sickish, too.

"Oh no," we said. "Pumpkin pie. We have to eat pumpkin pie."

But then HA!

Good old Lennie came to the rescue!

'Cause he already had the whole thing figured out!

"Don't worry, everyone! I've got a *plan*!" he said very excited.

He pointed to the back of the room.

"We've got a giant cleanup sink back there, remember?" he said.

All of us looked at the cleanup sink.

"So?" we said.

Lennie grinned. "So if anyone makes us eat pie, we'll just put it in our mouths . . . then run to the cleanup sink . . . and quick spit it out!" he said.

All of Room One thought for a second.

Then *WHEW!*

A big breath of relief whooshed right out of us.

'Cause spitting pie in the cleanup sink is *a genius,* of course!

We started smiling again.

Hurray for Lennie!

That guy thinks of everything.

10

Naming Stuff

All of us skipped back to our seats.

Principal walked to the front of the room.

And he saw our Thankful List on the board.

We had added more stuff on Tuesday afternoon. So now it was twenty whole items long!

Principal read the list out loud.

1. CRANBERRY JELLY IN A CAN
2. EXPLODING BISCUITS

3. NIPSY DOODLES
4. RAINBOW SPRINKLES
5. TOILET PAPER
6. MONEY
7. PHILIP JOHNNY BOB
8. POLICE SERGEANT CHUCK
9. SNAUSAGES
10. STINKY
11. GOOD OLD LARRY FROM LAST YEAR
12. COOKIES—BUT NOT THE COCONUT KIND
13. JOSÉ'S REMOTE CONTROL
14. LIGHTNING BUGS
15. THE BIG BOX OF 64 CRAYONS
16. PENGUINS
17. LENNIE'S WASHCLOTH PUPPET
18. WHIPPED CREAM THAT ROGER ACCIDENTALLY SQUIRTED IN HIS MOUTH BEFORE SCHOOL

After he finished reading, Principal smiled real big.

"Boys and girls, this is the most honest list we have ever had in the school contest," he said. "Thank you for telling us what children are *really* thankful for."

Lennie turned around and looked at May.

Then he did a big smirk.

"Nipsy Doodles rule," he said.

May turned his head back around.

Just then, we heard feet in the hallway.

And yay! Yay! Hurray!

Our favorite janitor came through the door!

"GUS VALLONY! IT'S GUS VAL-LONY!" I shouted real thrilled.

Gus Vallony is the nicest janitor in the whole entire world.

He was pushing a cart with a table and folding chairs on it.

I jumped up so he could see me.

"Gus Vallony! It's me! It's Junie B. Jones!" I yelled. "Did you hear we won the Thankful Contest? Did you see the blue ribbon on our door?"

I hurried to the front of the room. "What do you have there, Gus Vallony? Is that folding chairs for our feast today? 'Cause maybe I could help you with them!"

Gus Vallony did a chuckle at me.

"Well, Junie B. Jones! Don't you look nice today!" he said. "You're all dressed up like a Pilgrim girl."

I nodded. "Yes, I know," I said. "At first, I did not want to be a Pilgrim girl. And so me and Mother had a tussle behind the trash can. Only now I am hardly even sweaty. Plus also, I can spit pie in the cleanup sink. And so my whole entire mood got better."

Gus Vallony looked confused at me.

Principal looked confused, too.

Mr. Scary walked me back to my seat. And he said for me to *please stay put.*

After that, Principal helped Gus Vallony and Mr. Scary set up the table and chairs.

And wait till you hear this!

All of our guests had signed up to bring the feast food. So Room One didn't have to make a thing!

I tapped on my friend Herbert.

"What kind of food is your mother

bringing?" I asked. "My mother and my grandma Miller are bringing cranberry jelly."

Herbert turned around. "My mother has to work today. But my grandmother is bringing carrot sticks."

"Oh boy!" I said. "I love carrot sticks."

Lennie grinned. "Me too," he said. "My grandmother is coming to the feast. But she's a terrible cook. So I signed her up for napkins."

Sheldon heard us talking.

"My uncle Vern is coming with my grampa Ned Potts. And they're bringing Tater Tots!" he said.

I did a gasp at that delicious news.

"Yummy yum yum!" I said. "Tater Tots!"

May threw her head back.

"Pilgrims and Indians did *not* eat Tater Tots," she said real annoyed. "My mother is bringing the *real* kind of food that they ate at the first Thanksgiving."

She stood up at her desk. And she swung her long braid again.

"My mother is bringing squash . . . and beans . . . and stewed onions," she said real proud.

After that, Room One got very quiet.

We were thinking about stewed onions, I believe.

Then, one by one, we all turned around. And we looked at the cleanup sink again.

I glanced at Lennie. "That sink is going to get a real workout today," I said.

Just then, we heard more footsteps in the hall.

And YIPPEE! YIPPEE!

Our first Thanksgiving guest was here!

It was Lucille's richie nanna! And she brought her real, actual chef guy with her!

The chef guy was wearing a tall white hat. And a long apron. It was all the way to his knees, almost.

Also, he was carrying a giant silver tray with a shiny lid on the top.

He put the tray on the feast table. And he pulled off the lid.

And wowie wow wow!

It was the giantest turkey I ever saw!

We ran to the table.

"Whoa!" said Roger. "How much does that big boy weigh?"

"How much did it cost?" said Lennie.

"Can I have the drumstick?" asked Herb.

"What's his name?" said Sheldon.

The richie nanna started to sputter.
"Uh, oh dear. Well, let's see. I didn't really

shop for it myself, so I don't know what it weighs. Or what it costs. And, hmm . . . I don't think it has a name," she said.

She raised her eyebrows at the chef guy. "Does it?" she asked.

I thought for a second. Then I clapped my hands.

"*I've* got an idea! Let's name him Mr. Turkey Pants!" I said.

Then I laughed and laughed. And all of Room One laughed, too.

Names are always funnier if you add the word *pants* on the end of them.

My grampa Frank Miller taught me that lesson.

Just then, another guest came through the door.

It was Herbert's grandmother. And she had a big white bowl full of carrot sticks.

"Whoa! That is a lot of carrot sticks, madam!" I said.

Sheldon looked at me and grinned. "What's their name, Junie B.?" he asked.

I thought again.

"Their name is Mr. Crunchy Pants!" I said.

After that, all of us laughed even more.

Mr. Scary said *go back to our seats*.

"Boys and girls, I know it's fun to have our families at our Thanksgiving feast today. But we need to be on our best behavior for them, remember?"

His eyes zoomed in on me. "And, Junie B.? I'm pretty sure we're finished naming the food. Okay?"

I did a salute.

"Aye, aye, Captain," I said.

I am a hoot.

Just then, I turned my head, and I saw my mother come in with Grandma Helen Miller. And yippee! My grampa Frank Miller came, too!

They put a big bowl of jiggly cranberry jelly on the table.

"Hey! Look! It's Mr. Jiggle Pants!" I shouted.

Mr. Scary did a frown at me.

Mother and Grandma Miller frowned, too.

Grampa laughed real loud. Then Grandma poked him with her elbow.

I slid way down in my chair.

"Oops," I said. "Sorry."

Then I covered my mouth with my hand.

And I didn't name food for the rest of the day.

11

The Feast

May's mother was the last guest to come to our room.

She was carrying three bags of food.

I did a sniff.

Something did not smell delicious.

It was the stewed onions, I believe.

Also, it was the beans and squash.

My stomach did a flip-flop at those stinky smells.

I took some deep breaths to try to calm it down.

Here is a helpful hint. Deep breathing

does not work that good when you are smelling stink.

Finally, I said the word *bluck*. And I held my nose.

Mr. Scary snapped his fingers at me.

That meant *please let go of your nose,* I think.

After all the guests were sitting down, Mr. Scary said a welcome speech to them.

"Welcome, everyone! Welcome to our feast!" he said. "Room One would like to thank you for bringing this delicious food to help us celebrate Thanksgiving."

After that, he gave the children a nod. And all of us shouted, "THANK YOU!"

A lot of rehearsing had gone into that.

"This is going to be a wonderful day," said Mr. Scary. "So please grab a plate. And let's get started."

We let our guests go first.

That is some kind of guest rule, apparently.

Room One lined up behind them.

Only too bad for me. 'Cause someone took the lid off the stewie pewie onions. And the smell almost knocked me down.

My stomach felt sickish and rumbly.

I hurried to the end of the food line.

Mr. Scary saw me go. But this time, he did not get mad.

Instead, he made a 'nouncement to all of the children.

"Boys and girls, today is a celebration of all the things we're thankful for. And—since each of us is thankful for different kinds of foods—just take the food you love the most. And enjoy every single bite."

All of us did a breath of relief.

Then things got even better!

Because Mr. Scary walked over to the supply closet. And he pulled out one more bag of food for our Thanksgiving feast.

And its name was . . .

"NIPSY DOODLES!" shouted Lennie. "MR. SCARY BROUGHT NIPSY DOO-DLES!"

He ran to Mr. Scary and did a high five.

After that, we could not *wait* to get our plates of food!

It was the tastiest Thanksgiving dinner I ever even ate!

I had turkey! And carrot sticks! And Nipsy Doodles! And cranberry jelly!

Herb had turkey! And carrot sticks! And two giant plops of applesauce!

Lennie just had Nipsy Doodles and that's all. Plus also, he took four napkins.

"It will make my grandmother feel good," he said.

After we finished eating, all of the children walked around the room. And we thanked our families for the food they brought.

"Thank you for your crunchy carrot sticks," I said to Herb's grandmother.

"Thank you for your hugie, big turkey," I said to Lucille's richie nanna.

"Your napkins were delicious," I said to Lennie's grandmother.

After that, I thanked Mother and Grandma Miller for the cranberry jelly.

Then Grampa Frank Miller picked me up. And he spun me all around real happy.

Frank would be fun in my real, actual class, I believe.

After we got done with our thank-yous, Mr. Scary said he had one more happy surprise for us.

Then he looked in the hallway.

And he did a nod.

And guess who came in next?

"MRS. GUTZMAN!" I shouted. "IT'S MRS. GLADYS GUTZMAN!"

Mrs. Gutzman is the bestest lunch lady in the whole entire world!

I sprang out of my seat.

"HELLO, GLADYS GUTZMAN! IT'S ME! IT'S JUNIE B. JONES!"

Mrs. Gutzman was holding two pie boxes in her hands.

She put them down and waved at me.

"Hello, Junie B. Jones! Hello, children!" she said. "Congratulations on winning the Thankful Contest!"

She took out a pumpkin pie. And she held it up for everyone to see.

"Boys and girls, I baked these pumpkin pies for you myself! And I used my own family recipe," she said. "These pies will just melt in your mouth!"

Lennie looked at me and rolled his eyes. "Mine will be melting in the cleanup sink," he said.

"Ditto," I said. *Ditto* is the grown-up word for *mine will be melting in the cleanup sink, too.*

Herb's face looked bluckish and sickish. "I just want to get it over with," he said.

Lennie nodded.

"Let's do it," he said. "Let's hurry up and get our pie. And then we'll do a quick spit in the cleanup sink. And it will be all over."

Mrs. Gutzman started dishing out the pie.

Me and Herb and Lennie took a deep breath.

Then we quick ran to the pie table.

And we each grabbed a plate.

And we ran to the cleanup sink speedy fast.

We looked at the pie and made sick faces.

Then we took another deep breath.

And . . . READY . . . SET . . . GO!

All of us shoved some pie in our mouths!

After that, we stood there very still. And we let it just sit there.

It felt cold and squishy.

I smacked my lips a little bit.

Herb and Lennie smacked their lips, too.

Then, one, two, three . . . *GULP!*

We swallowed our pie at the exact same time.

And wowie wow wow!

That stuff was *delicious,* I tell you!

My head had confusion in it.

"Wait. Hold it. I don't *get* it," I said. "I hate pumpkin pie. But *this* pumpkin pie tastes delightful."

Herb smacked some more.

"Yes," he said. "It *does* taste delightful."

Lennie did not talk.

He was busy licking his plate.

After he finished, he looked up and smiled.

"Mrs. Gutzman is magic!" he said.

All of us laughed real happy.

'Cause that was the answer. Gladys Gutzman *is* magic.

We hurried back to the pie table for seconds.

"Thank you, Gladys! Thank you! Thank you!" I said real loud. "This is the bestest first prize I ever ate!"

I ran and hugged her real happy.

Mrs. Gutzman did a chuckle.

Then she leaned down.

And she hugged me back.

And she said don't call her Gladys.

12

Happy Turkey Day!

After all the pie was gone, I threw my plate in Mr. Scary's trash can.

And oh dear! Oh dear! *That's* when I saw him! Philip Johnny Bob was *still* sitting on the desk with Police Sergeant Chuck!

And I had forgotten all about that guy!

I ran over and picked him up. Then I hugged him real tight.

"Philip!" I said. "How did I forget you? You have been sitting there for two whole days! And you did not have one thing to eat."

Philip nodded his head.

I know it, he said. *I would really like some cranberry jelly right now.*

I patted his softie head.

"I *know* you would, Phil. But you can't have cranberry jelly, remember?" I said. "We tried that last Thanksgiving. And you still have the cranberry stain on your mouth."

Phil quick wiped his face.

Oh yeah . . . right, he said.

He looked at the feast table again.

Is there anything I can eat over there? he said.

I did a sigh.

"I don't know, Phil," I said. "At home, I just shove a peanut up your trunk. But no one brought nuts to the feast today."

I pointed to the carrot sticks.

"What about those, Phil? Would you like me to put a carrot up your trunk?" I asked.

Phil shook his head no. *That would look gross,* he said.

I nodded. "Yes. You're right," I said. "It *would* look gross."

I looked around.

Then, all of a sudden, I spotted a *brand-new bag of Nipsy Doodles*! They were sitting on Mr. Scary's desk! And a Nipsy Doodle was just the right size for Phil!

I quick opened the bag. And I put a Doodle in his trunk.

YUM! said Philip. *This Doodle is delicious! Thank you, Junie B.! Thank you!*

Just then, a voice shouted in my ear.

Hey! Hold it! Those Doodles don't belong to you, mister! You are under arrest!

I quick spun around.

The voice was coming from May. But she was pointing to Police Sergeant Chuck.

She hurried to Mr. Scary's desk. And she quick picked him up.

And then *BOOM!*

Out of nowhere, Chuck bopped Phil in the head with his trunk.

You stole a Nipsy Doodle! And stealing is against the law! he said.

Then May tried to take the Doodle right out of Philip's trunk! But Philip ducked around her.

Everyone looked to see the commotion.

Mr. Scary frowned real big.

May started to holler.

"None of this is my fault!" she said. "Peanut Butter and Johnny has a Nipsy

Doodle in his trunk! And Junie B. stole it for him!"

I stamped my foot. "No, I did *NOT*!" I said. "Nipsy Doodles are part of our Thanksgiving feast! And feast food is for sharing."

May stamped her foot, too.

"But that wasn't *sharing* food, Junie Jones. That was a brand-new bag! And it belonged to Mr. Scary!"

Then May tried to pull Phil away from me.

But I pulled him back.

Plus Philip bopped Chuck on his head.

And then all of us got ready to wrestle.

Only before we could even get started, Mr. Scary jumped in between us. And he stopped us from bopping each other.

"Girls! Girls!" he said. "That's enough!

Have you forgotten that we have *guests*?"

Me and May looked at our guests.

May's mother was frowning at us.

Mother and Grandma Miller were frowning again, too.

I glanced at my grampa Frank Miller.

He did a wink.

That was refreshing.

Mr. Scary kept on talking.

"I really don't understand what gets into you girls when you pick up those elephants," he said. "It's such a puzzle to me."

I thought for a second.

Then I did a little shrug.

"I don't know why it's a puzzle," I said. "Me and May are just playing with our elephants. And elephants like to bop each other."

May nodded her head.

"Yes," she said. "That's what their trunks are for. Trunks are for bopping. That's how elephants play."

I thought some more.

Then I looked at May.

"Yeah, only maybe Mr. Scary doesn't *know* that, May," I said. "Maybe he doesn't *have* an elephant at home."

May did a pause.

"Oh. Right," she said. "I never thought of that."

She looked back at Mr. Scary. "Well, anyway . . . that's how elephants play," she said. "And so Junie Jones and I automatically know that."

I smiled. "Yes," I said. "We do."

Then—all of a sudden—*BLINK!*

A light bulb went off in my head!

I did a gasp.

"Mr. Scary, Mr. Scary! You were *right*!" I said. "Even though May and I are very different from each other, we both love elephants! And so *that* is how come we were almost being friends just now! 'Cause we have *something in common*! Just like the Pilgrims and the Native Americans!"

May looked curious at me.

"Yeah. But we're not really, *really* friends. Right, Junie Jones?" she said. "It was just this one time. Correct?"

"Correct!" I said back. "We can't be friends *forever*, May! That would be ridiculous! We don't even *like* each other!"

May got relief in her face.

"Whew. Okay. Good," she said. "Because I really like being different from you."

"I know it, May! I like being different from you, too," I said. "*Very* different."

May smiled.

I smiled back.

Then I tried to do a fist bump with her. But she did not see it coming. And I accidentally hit her in the arm.

"Ow!" she said.

"Sorry," I said.

May shrugged her shoulders. Then she rubbed it off.

After that, we both skipped to our seats with our elephants. And we hugged our elephants real tight.

It was a lovely moment, I think.

But—all of a sudden—it got interrupted by shouting.

I quick looked up.

It was Sheldon and Uncle Vern and Grampa Ned Potts.

"HAPPY TURKEY DAY! HAPPY TURKEY DAY!" they shouted real loud.

They were holding hands in the front of
the room.
   And they were doing three squeezes.
   All of the children stood up.
   We grinned from ear to ear.

"HAPPY TURKEY DAY!" we shouted
back.

Mr. Scary looked at Room One.

His face got beamy and proud.

He was thankful for us, I believe.

Don't miss these other great books by Barbara Park!

Rah! Rah! Rah!
Join the crowd.
Read these books
And laugh out loud!

BARBARA PARK is beloved by millions as the author of the *New York Times* bestselling Junie B. Jones series. She has won over forty children's book awards and has been featured in the *New York Times*, *USA Today*, and *Time* magazine. Twenty years after the world's funniest kindergartner debuted, Barbara says, "I've never been sure whether Junie B.'s fans love her in spite of her imperfections or because of them. Either way, she's gone out into the world and made more friends than I ever dreamed possible."

Barbara Park is also the author of award-winning middle-grade novels and picture books, including *Mick Harte Was Here*, *The Graduation of Jake Moon*, and *MA! There's Nothing to Do Here!* She and her husband, Richard, live in Arizona. Her family—which includes two of the handsomest little grandboys on the planet—lives nearby.

DENISE BRUNKUS'S entertaining illustrations have appeared in over fifty books. She lives in Massachusetts with her husband.